About the Author

Tristan J. Buckner is a Nashville born author, entrepreneur, and public speaker committed to empowering the overlooked and rebuilding lives through honesty, hustle, and healing. After serving 13 years in prison, he returned home not as a statistic, but as a solution—founding Buckner Live X-perience Youth Nonprofit and launching *The Felon's Guide*, To Integration Into The Professional Society...LESSONS ALONG THE WAY. (OnAmazon) a transformative resource for reentry and personal reinvention.

With a barbershop as his base and purpose as his compass, Tristan has mentored dozens of young men, spoken on reentry reform panels, and written his debut full-length work, *American Skin, Southern Soil*. His journey is one of redemption through service, rooted in hard truths and southern soul. Tristan continues to live and lead in Tennessee, shaping a new narrative for those who refuse to be counted out.

Dedication

For Ms. Mary Buckner—my mother, my foundation, and my forever strength. Your love never wavered, even when the world did. Your prayers followed me into the darkest places, and your faith carried me out of them. At 84, you are still the blueprint of resilience, grace, and sacrifice. This book is not just mine—it is ours. I honor you with every word, every page, every breath.

Foreword

By Loren Buckner

U.S. Army, Retired

When I look at my brother Tristan, I don't just see a man who came home—I see a man who came back with fire. This book is not just his story. It's a blueprint, a testament, and a battle cry for every man who's ever been buried under a label.

I had the honor of not only standing beside my brother in life but also giving him a piece of mine—a kidney. It wasn't just an organ. It was a symbol. Of brotherhood. Of rebuilding. Of choosing life over silence.

Tristan and I are only a year apart, but the paths we walked couldn't have been more different. Yet through it all—the distance, the war, the walls—we stayed linked by something stronger than circumstance: blood, and belief.

American Skin, Southern Soil is not a feel-good tale. It's a real-good one. It's raw, it's southern, and it's needed. This is more than a book. It's a movement. And I couldn't be prouder to say it began with my brother.

American Skin, Southern Soil

Chapter 1:
The Gate Opens

The sun didn't greet me. It was colder than I remembered, and freedom didn't feel like applause or celebration. It felt like concrete under my boots and silence in my chest. Thirteen years behind a wall that talked back every night, and now—just air. I walked out with two trash bags: one full of letters and drawings from a life paused, the other stuffed with Department of Corrections issued clothes I wouldn't wear in hell. The gate clanked shut behind me like it was happy to forget my name.

Loren leaned on his Dodge, arms crossed, head low. My brother hadn't aged much, but the tired in his eyes said different. We didn't hug. We didn't need to. He handed me a folded hoodie—black, heavy, no logos—and a small brown paper bag that smelled like something illegal. It was, a bacon sandwich. "Man, they let you out skinnier than you went in," he said, handing me the bag. "You look like time ain't ate nothin' but your patience."

I smiled, barely. "You still ugly."

He laughed. The kind of laugh brothers use to keep from crying.

The ride back into Nashville was quiet at first. I watched the skyline grow out of the morning fog like it didn't remember me either. Billboards. Condos. Churches. Fast food chains lined the streets like flags in conquered territory. Loren had a gospel station playing low, but I caught a few headlines on the radio: "New business grant approved for small businesses... felony exclusions apply." Another one about an opioid crisis. Another about a protest in Memphis. America hadn't changed, just shifted costumes. "You still cuttin'?" Loren finally asked.

"Yeah," I said. "That's all I got right now."

"You still got them hands though." He nodded. "Got a chair lined up?"

"Just me and a mirror in that backroom you gave me." I glanced over. "Clients gon' come?"

"Clients always come when they see blood in your knuckles and truth in your eyes."

He dropped me at the two-bedroom off Jefferson Street. Same place I used to visit before the charges, before the trial, before the label of felon carved itself into my identity like a permanent scar. The barbershop was in the back of the house—a 10x10 room with a cracked floor, secondhand chair, and a mirror with scratches across its reflection like it didn't want to show you everything.

I set up. Clipped the blades to my WAHLs. Placed a towel over the chair even though no one was coming today. Or maybe not tomorrow either. But I kept the clippers humming. Kept moving like the customers were just running late.

Then, the knock.

It was a teenager, probably 19. Skinny, anxious, eyes darting like he was used to bad news. I opened the door slow, unsure what the day would bring.

"You cut?" he asked.

"You got twenty dollars?"

He nodded.

I waved him in. As I draped the cape over his shoulders, he looked in the mirror and said, "You just get out?"

I paused. "Yeah."

He nodded slowly. "My pops still in. Got ten left on fifteen."

I didn't answer. Just started the fade.

The hum of the clippers took over. Each pass was a prayer. Each edge-up was an act of rebellion. In that chair, in that moment, I wasn't a felon—I was a craftsman. I wasn't on borrowed time—I was buying it back, one cut at a time.

That night, I sat alone in that backroom, grease under my nails and tired in my bones. No applause. No parades. Just one cut, one twenty-dollar bill, and one reminder: I was out—but not done.

Freedom had a price tag.

And I was just getting started.

Chapter 2:
Clippers and Convictions

The city said I couldn't cut hair out my own house.

Said I needed a commercial license, said I needed zoning, said I needed permission.

But I knew what they were really saying:

You need permission to be free.

They weren't gonna give that to me. So I took it.

I moved the chair to the front porch.

I cut on concrete. Wind blowing hair into the grass. Clients sat on crates and folding chairs until I could get them into my seat. I bought a canopy for rain. Got a Bluetooth speaker for jazz and gospel.

No walls? Fine. I didn't need walls to build a business. I needed consistency.

Loren came by on a Thursday with a brown envelope.

"LegalZoom packet," he said. "I started the LLC paperwork in your name."

I blinked. "For what business?"

He looked around. "*This* one. Buckner Cuts & Coaching."

"You added coaching?" I asked.

He smiled. "Barbershop therapy, man. You've been preaching all week. Might as well claim it."

And he wasn't lying. These chairs weren't just about fades. Men came to me broken, quiet, unsure.

One was fresh out, same as me. Didn't know how to talk to his teenage daughter.

Another one was thirty, never been arrested but carried guilt from years of hustling.

Then there was the preacher who didn't believe in forgiveness—until he sat in my chair

The clippers buzzed while we talked about God, about loss, about the system that didn't rehabilitate—it just rotated.

They didn't just leave with clean edges.

They left lighter.

I was left heavier.

But it was worth it.

Then came Mark.

White coat. Black man. Been a doctor twenty years. Walked up one afternoon with a cane and a kindness in his voice that felt familiar.

"I heard you cut and counsel," he said.

I nodded. "You need both?"

He laughed. "No. I want to help."

He told me about a youth clinic downtown. Said they needed barbers for a "confidence day." Haircuts for free. Talk to the kids. Be visible.

"I don't want you to just cut hair, Tristan," he said. "I want them to *see* you."

So I went.

First time I'd been in a school setting in over a decade. Posters of Harriet Tubman and Rosa Parks on the wall. Staff looking at me like I was undercover. But the kids? They lit up.

I cut ten boys that day. Each one asked questions—about prison, about dreams, about failure.

One boy, age 11, asked, "Did you lose your smile in jail?"

I paused. Clipped. "Nah," I said. "I found it when I got out."

That night, I sat with my clippers and a notebook.

I wrote Chapter 2 of my guide:

"Clippers ain't just tools—they're bridges."

Because that's what I was building. A way to cross from what I'd done to who I was becoming.

No zoning board could shut *that* down.

Chapter 3:
Mary's Eyes

I didn't visit Mama the first day I got out. Not because I didn't want to.

Because I didn't know how to look her in the eye.

Mary Buckner was a praying woman. Eighty-four years old, fire still in her bones. She raised three boys on Social Security checks and faith. One dead. One disappeared. And me—back from a cage.

I showed up on a Sunday. Sun high, gospel humming from inside. She lived in the same brick duplex off Buchanan Street. Same plastic flowers on the porch. Same smell of fried cabbage and Lysol.

I knocked.

She opened. Eyes wide. Wrinkles deeper. Arms thin but strong. She didn't say anything. Just stared.

"You gon' hug me or call the police?" I joked.

She slapped my arm. Hard. Then hugged me tighter than any cell door ever closed.

Inside was like time paused. Same brown couch. Same picture of Martin and Malcolm side by side. Same lace tablecloth with yellowing corners. She moved slow now, but her voice was sharp as ever.

"You eat?"

"No, ma'am."

"Sit."

She made a plate without asking—fried chicken, cornbread, mustard greens. I hadn't tasted soul like that in 13 years. I almost cried into the macaroni.

"You still believe in God?" she asked out of nowhere.

I chewed slow. Swallowed hard.

"I believe I'm still here," I said. "That's gotta count."

She nodded. "That's a start."

We talked like we didn't lose years. Like visits and letters had kept us whole. But they hadn't. There were cracks.

"You still cuttin'?" she asked.

"Trying."

She handed me an envelope. Inside: two crisp hundreds.

"What's this?"

"Seed money."

"Mama—"

"Boy, I didn't raise no beggar, but I sure as hell didn't raise no fool who says no to help."

Later, she pulled out an old album.

"You remember this?"

Photos of me in high school. State championship jersey. Graduation picture. One of me at the church cutting Deacon Patterson's hair on the back steps.

"You been a barber since God was giving out callings," she said.

"Yeah," I said. "Then I got called by the court system."

Her eyes didn't flinch. "You made a mistake, baby. But you not your record."

As I left, she grabbed my hand.

"Tristan," she said, voice trembling. "Don't let 'em break you again."

"I won't."

"And don't hide. We done hiding in this family."

I walked home thinking about her voice. About the strength it took to love a son through bars. About how her love was a mirror—I just had to look in it long enough to see myself clear again.

That night, I wrote Chapter 3 of the guide: "You gotta forgive yourself before anybody else can."

Chapter 4:
Red Tape in Red States

The city said I needed permission.

The state said I needed patience.

But what I needed was a damn chance.

Tennessee, for all its beauty, wore its red like a warning label. Republican-controlled. Conservative-core. Laws stacked like bricks— none of them built to house Black dreams. Especially not felons trying to start something clean.

I walked into the Metro Codes office with my head high and papers in hand. Business license form. Zoning request. Application for a barber's permit tied to a home address.

The woman behind the counter looked like she'd already said no to ten men like me that day.

"You the owner?" she asked.

"Yes, ma'am."

"Felony on record?

I hesitated. "Yes, ma'am."

She sighed. "Then we got a problem."

They didn't outright say no. They just made "yes" a maze.

Background check. Court transcript. Letter of explanation.

A hearing.

Three signatures.

Two more fees.

It felt like they were hoping I'd quit before I started.

I called my friend Isaac—Professor Isaac Langston from Fisk University. He taught criminal justice and policy. We met at a reentry conference years ago. He believed in redemption. He believed in me.

"They'll bury you in paperwork, Tristan," he said over coffee. "It's not about the law—it's about fatigue. They want to exhaust you."

"So what do I do?"

"You outlast the noise. You document everything. You make them tell you no in writing. And when they do, you make sure the community knows why."

So I started posting.

Screenshots. Letters. Emails.

"Filed for a license today. Got asked if I 'deserve' to run a business."

"Day 5: Still waiting on a callback. But I'm still cutting."

The posts got attention.

Local barber pages reshared it.

Then a city councilman inboxed me. Black, mid-40s, tired of being quiet.

"Let's talk," he wrote.

We met at a soul food spot off Charlotte. He wore a tailored suit and ate cornbread like it healed something in him.

"I read your posts," he said. "You got eyes on you now."

"Good," I said. "I want them to see."

He leaned forward. "But if you're gonna fight, fight smart. Get allies. Show up at meetings. Use their language against them."

I nodded. I wasn't trying to be a martyr. I was trying to build a business.

That night, I spoke at a zoning board hearing. My first public speech since I was sentenced in '94.

"I'm not asking for a handout," I said. "I'm asking for a fair shot."

I told them about the porch cuts. The kids. The conversations. The healing.

I told them about my guidebook.

About my mother.

About the mirror I was trying to fix in my life.

Some nodded. Some avoided eye contact. One old white man scribbled something and didn't look up once.

They didn't decide that night. Said they'd "review the petition."

But I'd already won something.

My story was out there.

And I wasn't hiding.

Chapter 5:
Faith on the Fade

The first time I thought about quitting, I was lining up a preacher.

Reverend Johnson. Sixty-something. Big silver beard. Smelled like peppermint and old leather. He sat down, stared in the mirror, and said, "Make me look like I still believe in God."

I laughed. "Razor that strong don't exist."

He didn't smile. "A man don't preach thirty years and not lose something."

I took the cape and wrapped it around him. As I oiled the clippers, he kept talking.

"Do you believe you're forgiven?" he asked.

"By who?"

"Start with yourself."

I paused. Looked at his eyes in the mirror. "Some days."

That cut took forty-five minutes.

Not because his hair was tough. Because the air was heavy.

He told me he stopped preaching after his son OD'd. Said the church folks gave him casseroles, not comfort.

"I've buried hope," he said, "but I still keep the shovel just in case I need to dig it back up."

I edged him sharp. Faded him clean. And when he looked at himself afterward, he cried. Quiet. One tear.

I said, "Looks like you found something."

He nodded. "And so did you."

That night I sat alone in the shop. Lights low. Clippers buzzing like a lullaby. I thought about all the people sitting in that chair.

It wasn't just about hair.

It was about faith.

Faith that your story wasn't over.

Faith that clean lines could mean a clean start.

Faith that redemption ain't a sermon — it's a service you give every day.

The next morning, I woke up to a DM from a woman named Tasha. Social worker. Said her nonprofit was working with reentry programs. Said they needed a speaker — somebody who lived it.

"You come talk to our young men?" she wrote.

I'd never spoken in public outside a courtroom. But I said yes.

The day of the talk, I wore a hoodie and fresh sneakers. No suit. No tie. Just truth.

Room full of teenagers—some with bracelets, some with baby faces. They laughed when I walked in. Whispered.

But then I spoke.

Told them about the first night back. About cutting hair on porches. About rejection letters and zoning violations and my mama's stare.

I told them the dream don't come with blueprints—but if you listen close, you can hear the rhythm of your rebuild.

When I finished, nobody clapped. But one kid stood up.

He said, "You make me think maybe I ain't ruined."

That was the loudest amen I ever heard.

Chapter 6:
The Felon's Guide

The day I realized I was an author, not just a barber, I didn't have a desk. Just a kitchen table, half a notebook, and a scar across my record that no job application wanted to see.

I wrote the title across the top of the page: "The Felon's Guide to Not Dying Poor."

It sounded like a joke.

But it wasn't.

It was a blueprint. A manual. A truth bomb for people like me — branded, boxed out, breathing but not really living. I wasn't writing to inspire. I was writing to survive. And maybe, to teach someone else how to do the same.

The first section was called "Rebuilding Without Permission."

Because I had to. I had no cosign. No investors. No safe zone. Just clippers, courage, and a constant sense of being watched.

I wrote about getting my first client after release.

About zoning letters and legal hoops.

About applying for a business license 4 times, denied twice, "pending" forever.

I wrote:

"The system ain't broken. It's working exactly how it was built—to make us give up."

Mark stopped by that evening.

He dropped a used laptop on my table. Dell. Beat up. Slow. Perfect.

"Figured your book deserved better than pen and pad," he said.

I nodded, grateful.

He leaned against the fridge. "Tristan, you realize you're writing something nobody else can?"

"What's that?"

"A map out of hell from somebody who made it back."

I created a table of contents:

Rebuilding Credit with $7.62 in Your Pocket

Making Room in a Room You Don't Own

Public Speaking When They Think You Can't Read

LLCs, Side Hustles & Not Catching Charges

Parenting from the Stain of Your Past

I wasn't a preacher. I wasn't a professor. But I had something to say.
And that made me dangerous.

A week later, I printed the first chapter and read it aloud in a community
center. Tasha from the nonprofit had set it up. Twenty chairs. Eleven
people showed. Six stayed the whole time.

But when I finished, a man in the back stood up. "Where can I buy
this?" he asked.

I laughed. "I'm still writing it."

"Well, hurry up," he said. " 'Cause I need the next chapter."

That night, I put the manuscript in a folder. Scribbled a note on top:

"This ain't about being perfect. It's about proving you're not done."

I looked in the mirror, held up the folder, and said out loud —

"You are an author now."

And for the first time, I believed it.

Chapter 7:
Ghosts of the Yard

The clink of a door still got to me.

Didn't matter if it was a cabinet or a truck tailgate. If it slammed, my body flinched. That noise didn't leave with my sentence. Neither did the shadows.

Prison don't just stay behind bars.

It moves into your muscles.

It whispers when you try to sleep.

It watches you when you think you're alone.

One night, I woke up sweating. No nightmare. Just silence so loud it sounded like yelling. I sat up, heart pounding, expecting roll call. Flashlights. Keys jangling.

But there was no flashlight.

No CO.

Just the sound of Loren snoring in the next room and wind brushing the window.

Still, I couldn't sleep. So I got up, grabbed the clippers, and started sharpening them. That was the ritual. That was what kept the ghosts at bay.

Some ghosts came with names. One of them was Tank. Big dude from Memphis. Life sentence. Never smiled. He carved chess pieces out of soap and once told me, "Every move outside that board's a trap. Make one wrong move and you're dead. In here or out there."

Tank died three months before I was released.

Not by violence. By the silence.

Stopped eating. Stopped talking. Stopped mattering.

One day, his body just gave up before his clock did.

That's when I promised myself I'd never shrink into nothing.

There was Curtis, too. Younger than me. Did five years for stealing car stereos. Had bars tattooed on his forearm, like he'd branded himself before the state could.

He used to say, "If we don't laugh in here, we'll lose language."

We laughed until he got jumped by three dudes from another pod.

No warning. No reason.

Just hierarchy in action.

I heard he survived. But I never saw him again.

These men weren't friends.

They were reminders.

Of how close I came to becoming invisible.

Of what waited for me if I ever slipped.

That's why I kept my clippers sharp.

Because it gave my hands purpose.

And purpose kept the ghosts quiet.

One day, I told Mark about the dreams. About Tank. About Curtis. About the silence that never fully left.

"You think I'm broken?" I asked.

He shook his head. "No. I think you're still healing."

"How long that take?"

He looked out the window. "As long as it takes."

That night, I added a new chapter to my guide:

"Some days you just survive. That's enough."

Because not every chapter ends in victory.

Some just end with you still here.

And that's the win.

Chapter 8:
Speaking in Chains

The first time I stepped on stage to speak, I didn't feel like a leader. I felt like an exhibit. The room smelled like lemon cleaner and polished wood. A gymnasium repurposed for "reentry inspiration." Folding chairs lined up in front of a mic duct-taped to a cracked stand. I stood behind a folding table, hands trembling, notes in my pocket I knew I wouldn't read.

The audience?

Teenagers. Some on probation. Some caught skipping school. Some just dragged in by caseworkers. All of them with eyes that had seen too much.

Tasha gave the intro. "This is Tristan Buckner. Father. Barber. Businessman. Author."

Author. That still hit weird in my ears.

She stepped aside, nodded. My cue.

I grabbed the mic. It squeaked. I looked at the crowd and forgot everything I was gonna say.

So I just told the truth.

"I did thirteen years for a mistake I made when I thought surviving was more important than living. I came out with a record, a reputation, and a whole lot of nothing."

A few heads looked up. Some didn't.

"But I also came out with clippers. And a decision."

I told them about the porch cuts.

About zoning boards and rejection letters.

About my mama's eyes.

About writing a book not because I had answers — but because I couldn't keep swallowing the questions.

I said, "They gonna tell you who you are every day. System, cops, schools, screens. They'll define you if you let 'em. But you still got the pen."

One kid stood up in the back. Baggy hoodie. No notebook. Just attitude. "You ever wanna go back?" he asked.

The room froze.

I looked at him dead in the eye. "Every time I'm scared I won't make it out here."

Silence.

"But then I remember what back feels like. That smell. That sound. That silence. And I keep going, even when I don't believe I can."

He sat down.

I kept going.

Afterward, a boy with tears in his eyes came up to me.

"My brother just got locked up," he said. "He cut hair too."

I pulled out a set of clippers from my bag and handed them to him.

He blinked. "These yours?"

"Not anymore. They yours now. Keep your brother sharp 'til he come home."

That night, I changed the title of my guide.

Not just *The Felon's Guide*.

Now it read: *The Free Man's Manual*. Because that's what I was doing. Teaching others how to walk with weight and still move like they meant to.

Chapter 9:
Barbershop Politics

The barbershop ain't just where fades get cleaned up.

It's where truths get aired out.

And in Nashville, it's where grown men talk like it's a pulpit, a courtroom, and a battlefield—all in the same hour.

I moved into a small storefront on the edge of North Nashville.

Loren helped me scrape the old name off the window.

We painted:

Buckner Cuts & Coaching

Sharp on the outside, real on the inside.

It wasn't fancy. One chair. One cracked mirror. One set of clippers.

But it was mine.

No zoning violations this time.

All paperwork signed. All permits clean.

I opened the door, flipped the sign to "Walk-ins Welcome," and waited.

My first client walked in wearing a suit and a scowl. "I heard you a felon," he said, sitting down.

"I heard you got a receding hairline," I replied.

He laughed. "We gon' get along just fine."

He was a school principal.

Had opinions on everything—parenting, politics, punishment.

"You know what your problem is?" he asked as I clipped.

I waited.

"You believe people can change. That's cute, but this state don't care about redemption."

I didn't argue. I just lined him up so sharp he tipped me extra.

Then came Marcus. Uber driver. Part-time rapper. Told me he used to sell dope but now sold T-shirts online.

"Progress," he said. "Different hustle, same pressure."

He talked about cops pulling him over for tint, for tags, for "matching a description." He said being Black in the South felt like a job he never applied for, but couldn't quit.

Every cut came with a conversation.

Single dads. Convicted mothers. Brothers who served in Iraq and came home to a city that didn't serve them back.

And me?

I just cut and listened.

But one day, I talked.

It was a Friday.

Crowded. Music playing low.

A debate sparked—welfare, crime, "personal responsibility."

I let it ride until somebody said:

"Most of y'all locked yourselves up."

I put the clippers down. Turned the music off.

"You think accountability means shutting up and taking what they give us?" I said. "That ain't growth. That's guilt talking. We got rights. We got voices. If all we do is cut each other down, we doing their job for them."

The room got quiet.

Then one man clapped. Then two.

Then it was back to business.

That night, I put a chalkboard in the shop.

Wrote at the top:

Today's Topic: What Needs to Change?

By the end of the week, it was full.

Education Access

Reentry housing

Health insurance

Us. We need to change too

The shop had become more than a hustle. It was a headquarters for truth. For growth. For revolution. One lineup at a time.

Chapter 10:

Enemy at the Zoning Board

The first time I got called "a threat" in a public meeting, I was wearing a button-down shirt and holding a clipboard.

They didn't say it with those words.

But they said it with the way they looked at me.

That day, I stood in front of the Nashville Zoning Appeals Board—again. Not to fight them this time. But to ask for expansion. I wanted to open a second space. A bigger one. Closer to the East Side. One more chair, a couple young barbers, a little room in the back for coaching and book talks.

I was thinking future. They were thinking fear.

"Mr. Buckner, your record is still active in our system," one of the board members said, flipping papers like he didn't know my name but knew every letter of my charges.

"Yes, sir," I replied. "And my business license is active too. So is my tax ID. So are the youth I mentor every week."

He cleared his throat. "We're just concerned with the precedent this might set."

"Precedent?" I asked.

"For allowing certain individuals to operate in certain districts."

There it was. "Certain individuals."

Translation: Black. Felon. Unapologetically visible.

I didn't yell. I didn't flinch. I did what I always did—stood tall and used my story.

"I'm not here for charity," I told them. "I'm not asking for handouts. I'm asking for space. Space to give young men a vision of something different. You want to talk precedent? Let's set one where redemption isn't a threat, but a resource."

They didn't answer. Just shuffled papers.

But a few folks in the room clapped. Some stood. A woman from a local community group took notes. A journalist in the back scribbled every word.

And that was when I knew—

Whether they approved it or not,

I had already expanded.

That night, my inbox exploded.

Messages from people I didn't know.

"Heard what you said. We need more of you."

"I'm a teacher. Can I bring students to your shop?"

"I work with reentry. Can we partner?"

Even better. One woman wrote: "I've got a building. Cheap lease. No board approval needed. Let's talk."

So I talked. And three weeks later, *Buckner Cuts East* opened with two chairs, a mural of Malcolm and Nipsey on the wall, and a laminated poster of the zoning letter taped to the bathroom door.

I kept it there as a reminder:

They tried to stall me with red tape.

But I used it to tie up my next move.

Chapter 11:
The Mentor Mirror

Sometimes, the hardest part of teaching is seeing yourself in the student.

It was a Thursday afternoon when Devon walked in.

Seventeen. Skinny. Quiet. Hoodie up, eyes down.

Didn't say much—just sat in the chair like the world owed him silence.

"You want a fade?" I asked.

He shrugged. "Whatever."

That "whatever" told me everything. He didn't care how he looked.

He didn't expect to matter.

I started cutting. Slow, steady strokes. The kind I give when I know I'm not just fixing hair—I'm trying to reach something underneath.

"You in school?" I asked.

He didn't answer.

"You working?"

Another shrug.

I glanced in the mirror. He was watching me—not my hands. My face.

"I got locked up at 17," I said. "Just like you."

That made him blink. A flicker of interest.

"Didn't think I'd live past 25. Now I'm here giving sharp lines and life lessons."

He cracked the smallest smirk. "You sound like my PO."

"Nah," I said. "Your PO gets paid to watch you. I'm just trying to keep you from disappearing."

After the cut, I didn't charge him. Just handed him a card. "Come back next week. I'll teach you how to hold these clippers."

He stared. "For real?"

"Only rule is you gotta show up."

He came back.

Not on time. Not clean. But he came.

Week by week, he got better. Lines got tighter. Posture got straighter. The mirror started showing someone he didn't hate.

Then he started bringing friends.

Then he started asking questions.

"How do I start an LLC?"

"What's credit?"

"What's a write-off?"

I saw myself in him. Not just who I was.

Who I could've been, if somebody handed me clippers instead of cuffs.

I told him everything I wish someone had told me:

Mistakes don't make you unworthy.

Being loud doesn't mean being heard.

Survival is basic—but creation is power.

One night, he stayed late after the shop closed. Sweeping up, wiping chairs. He said, "Mr. Buckner... you ever scared people still see you as what you were?"

I looked him in the mirror and answered, "Every day. But I'm not in the reflection to please them. I'm here to remind myself who I am now."

That night, I wrote Chapter 11 of my book: "If you want to lead, you gotta first learn to reflect."

Because a mirror ain't just for looking sharp.

It's for recognizing who still needs to heal—and being brave enough to guide them there.

Chapter 12:
Side Hustles and Scar Tissue

You can't survive in the South on one hustle.

Not when you're Black. Not when you're branded. Not when the system's watching like it hopes you blink first.

So I learned to diversify my grind.

The barbershop paid the bills — barely.

Some weeks I cut twenty heads, some weeks I cut two.

But the truth was, I needed more than clippers.

I needed layers.

So I started selling my book out the trunk of my car.

The Free Man's Manual — printed 50 copies with my last $300.

Hand-stapled. Paper-thin. But it was real.

Word spread faster than the ink could dry.

I started speaking again. Youth centers, churches, men's circles, Zoom panels.

No stage too small.

No honorarium too light.

One day, I spoke at a reentry workshop at Tennessee State University.

Afterward, a white man in a fleece vest approached me. "You ever thought about turning your book into a course?" he asked.

I blinked. "A what?"

"A curriculum. Felon leadership. Barber-based rehabilitation. LMS platform."

I laughed. "You sound like a grant proposal."

He handed me a card. "Exactly."

I didn't trust him at first. But the more I researched, the more I realized: White folks wrote programs about us all the time. But rarely *with* us. Never *as* us.

So I wrote a proposal. Built a plan. Filmed myself cutting and coaching. Titled the course: "Recreate: Cut Your Way Into Purpose."

The idea? Teach returning citizens how to build identity and income from something real.

No theory. No sugar. Just tools.

I submitted the grant.

Three months later, I got the call

Approved.

$20,000 pilot project.

Two community partners.

Fifty students.

I cried like the little boy I locked away in me years ago.

But it wasn't all clean.

With every step forward, the scar tissue pulled.

Old friends resurfaced.

Some cheered.

Some resented.

"You different now," one of them said. "You think you better?"

I looked him in the eye. "Nah. I just got tired of being stuck."

That night, I looked at my reflection—shirt sweaty, voice hoarse, inbox full.

I didn't see a barber.

I didn't see a felon.

I saw a builder.

A blueprint in motion.

And I wrote in my guide: "Every scar tells a story. But not every story ends in pain."

Chapter 13:

Between the Lines

There's something sacred about a lineup.

It's the part where everything gets defined.

The edge. The outline. The shape.

It's where the blur ends and the sharpness begins.

That's how I started seeing my life:

Between the lines.

One morning, an old head came into the shop—Mr. Leon.

Vietnam vet. Black fists tattooed on his forearms.

He sat down and didn't say much at first.

But when I started shaping his edge, he spoke: "You know they watchin' you, right?"

I paused. "Who?"

"Everybody. The city. The state. The ones who don't believe you clean."

I nodded. "I know."

"Good," he said. "Stay sharp. They always looking for a slip."

That hit harder than it should've.

Because I knew he was right.

Freedom wasn't free—it was rented.

And the payment was performance.

Every interaction had an audience.

Every misstep felt like proof.

So I tightened up.

My books. My language. My circle.

No more side talks with people still halfway in the game.

No more cutting corners, literally or metaphorically.

But even as I stayed between the lines, I realized...

There was no map for this.

No guidebook for Black men rebuilding under a microscope.

So I kept writing.

Not just in the guide.

In journals. On sticky notes. On my phone in the middle of the night.

I wrote what I couldn't say out loud—

"I'm tired."

"Sometimes I miss the structure of prison."

"I hate that I second guess every sentence I say in public."

"I want to feel free without having to prove I deserve it."

Then one day a kid I mentored came to the shop. Devon—sharp now, confident, cutting on weekends.

He asked me, "What do I do when I feel like the world's still waiting for me to mess up?"

I told him: "Live loud anyway. Be honest anyway. Keep cutting anyway. You ain't just walking the line—you redefining it."

That night, I wrote Chapter 13 of the book: "Freedom ain't just movement—it's definition. Define yourself before they do it for you."

Because staying between the lines is survival.

But sometimes?

You gotta redraw the damn lines.

Chapter 14:
Legacy in Progress

Legacy don't wait until you die.

It builds in real time.

In the cracks.

In the conversations.

In the moments you almost quit but don't.

I was at the shop late one night, sweeping up hair and prepping for a Monday class. Devon was in the back going over clippers with another young kid—Jalen. Fourteen. Fresh out the system after a juvie stint. Didn't smile much. Still walked like he expected someone to snatch the light from him at any second.

Devon was showing him how to level a taper.

"He holdin' the clippers like they a weapon," Devon said, smirking.

"They are," I replied from the front. "But we use 'em to protect peace now."

Jalen didn't say anything. But he was listening.

The next morning, I woke up to a text from Mark. "You need to trademark that course title ASAP. Word's gettin' around."

I didn't even know where to start. But I knew what that meant— progress had weight now. Real movement. Real pressure.

So I did what I always did: reached out to someone smarter than me.

Isaac walked me through the forms. Tasha linked me to a Black-owned trademark attorney. I filed the paperwork. Paid the fees.

And in that moment, *Buckner Recreate LLC* became more than a hustle. It became a legacy brand.

I thought about my daughter. She was sixteen now. We spoke more. Not perfect. But building.

She said, "Daddy, you famous now?"

I laughed. "Not even close."

"You on YouTube though."

I didn't know she was watching.

"I saw your talk," she said. "You ain't like those speakers who be frontin'. You talk like you actually hurt before."

I didn't cry. But I damn sure felt it.

Legacy don't always wear a cape.

Sometimes it walks into a barbershop on a Tuesday and sees their daddy speaking truth and doesn't flinch.

Sometimes it's a kid holding a pair of clippers like they holding the key to something they never thought they'd touch.

Sometimes it's your name on a trademark application you never thought you'd be able to afford.

That night, I didn't write a guide chapter.

I wrote a letter.

"To whoever reads this next:

You ain't here by mistake.

Every struggle, every scar, every side-eye moment you survived—

That's your blueprint.

Use it.

Live it.

Leave something behind that ain't just survival—it's structure."

Chapter 15:

The Sharpest Edge

Some say the sharpest blade is a straight razor.

But for me?

It's focus.

By the time *Buckner Cuts* had two chairs and a full schedule, I realized something—

I wasn't building a barbershop.

I was building a movement.

But with every new client, every event, every speech—I also felt the pull.

More visibility meant more opinions.

More praise.

More pressure.

And more people waiting for me to slip.

I got a call from a podcast.

Big platform. National reach.

They wanted me to come on and talk about reform, redemption, race, "and how a former felon made it."

That last part hit weird.

I didn't make it.

I was making it.

There's a difference.

But I said yes. Because I knew the story wasn't just mine anymore.

The interview dropped and blew up.

Thousands of plays. Shares. DMs. Opportunities.

One woman messaged me: "My son inside. Your story gave me hope for him."

Another: "I'm a parole officer. Your clip made me change how I talk to my caseload."

And then one I'll never forget: "I'm 17. I was about to take a plea. But I think I still got a future."

That was the moment I understood:

The sharpest edge ain't the clippers. It's the truth.

Spoken. Written. Lived.

But that edge cuts both ways.

With growth came scrutiny.

Someone sent a complaint to the city.

Anonymous.

Said I was "operating outside the scope of my license."

Said I was "using my story for personal gain."

Said I was "dangerous."

I called my lawyer.

We handled it. Nothing stuck.

But it reminded me—this path don't stop testing you just because you're on it.

It tests harder.

Because the higher you climb, the more visible your shadow becomes.

That night, I stood in front of the mirror.

Fresh haircut. Clean lineup.

Eyes tired. Mind sharp.

And I whispered to myself: "You ain't done. Keep cutting."

"They gon' come for you. Stay sharper."

Chapter 16:
The Father Chair

I didn't know how to be a father when I got out.

Thirteen years is a whole childhood.

You miss first steps.

First words.

Report cards.

Band-aids.

Back talk.

You miss trust.

My daughter's name is Alana.

When I went in, she was three.

When I came home, she was sixteen.

She stood on Mama's porch when I first saw her again.

Taller. Eyes like mine. Mouth like her mother's.

She didn't smile.

She didn't hug.

She just said, "Hi."

That "hi" hit like a sentence.

I didn't press.

I let her come to me.

Slow.

I started with texts. Then weekend meetups.

I let her talk. Let her ask questions.

I answered without dressing things up.

Yes, I did time.

Yes, I missed everything.

Yes, I hurt her.

Yes, I wanted to be better.

One Saturday, she came to the shop.

Hair braided. Hoodie on.

"You ever cut a girl before?" she asked.

"Only ones who let me."

She sat in the chair. Looked in the mirror. "I don't need a cut. Just wanted to see your world."

That hit.

I put the clippers down. Pulled out the mirror. Turned the chair to face me.

"This chair? This ain't just about cuts. It's about truth. What do *you* need?"

She stared. Swallowed.

"I need to know you won't leave again."

Silence.

I reached in the drawer, pulled out the same old clippers I used on my first cut since coming home.

I handed them to her.

"Keep these. If I ever go back to being the man I was, I want you to hand 'em back and remind me who I said I was gonna be."

She took them. Held them close.

Didn't cry.

Didn't run.

Just nodded.

And that day, she became part of my legacy.

Not because I earned it.

But because I chose not to lie to her anymore.

That night, I wrote Chapter 16 of the guide: "Forgiveness ain't a gift. It's a language. And you better learn to speak it before you lose the people worth translating for."

Chapter 17:
Three Cuts Ahead

Barbering teaches you more than how to fade.

It teaches strategy.

Patience.

Adaptability.

You gotta see the cut three moves ahead.

Just like life.

One Thursday morning, I had three back-to-back walk-ins.

The first was a high school senior prepping for prom.

Nervous, jittery, heart on his sleeve.

The second, a parolee two weeks out—quiet, twitchy, hands shaking when he handed me the money.

The third, a middle-aged Black businessman in a three-piece suit who said, "I just need to look like I don't carry all this stress."

Three men. Three cuts.

Three different types of survival.

As I cut each one, I realized: Barbers are more than stylists.

We're surgeons, strategists, and sometimes, soul savers.

We hear things clients don't tell therapists.

We see shifts in their energy before their own people do.

And we adapt—always thinking a few strokes ahead.

That week, I started sketching out a mentorship model.

Three levels:

Cutting for income – The hustle.

Cutting for healing – The heart work.

Cutting for legacy – Teaching others how to build their own chairs.

I called it "The Three Cut Principle."

I launched a free class on Instagram Live.

Had five viewers the first week. Then ten. Then fifty.

By week five, I had over 200 tuning in—some from different states.

DMs flooded in.

"Can I intern?"

"Can you review my fade?"

"Do you do one-on-one coaching?"

The hustle had matured into a platform.

One message hit different. From a young barber in Mississippi: "I almost quit last month. Your IG saved me. I didn't know felons could do what you're doing. You gave me blueprint and belief."

That night, I sat with a fresh cut in the mirror and said to myself: "You ain't a felon trying to cut no more. You're a builder teaching others how to shape themselves."

Then I wrote: "It's not about the cut you make today. It's about how it shapes the ones that follow."

Chapter 18:
The Price of Quiet

There's a silence that cuts deeper than a straight razor.

It's the silence of trying to do everything right

—yet still feeling like it ain't enough.

I hit a stretch where things were steady.

The shop had a rhythm.

The classes were booked.

The guide was moving online.

Even my daughter called twice a week now.

From the outside? I looked like a success story.

But inside?

I was tired.

See, nobody talks about the weight of being *the one who made it*—even a little.

Once you wear that crown, folks stop checking in on you.

They stop asking if you need anything.

Because "you good now," right?

One night, I closed the shop early.

No music. No phone.

I sat in the barber chair, alone, staring at my own reflection.

That mirror—the one I used to sharpen other people—now showed me someone unraveling.

Not from failure.

From expectation.

Mark came by the next morning, unexpected. He took one look at me and said, "You been holding your breath again, huh?"

I nodded.

He sat in the chair. Didn't ask for a cut.

Just said, "Talk."

So I did.

About burnout.

About guilt.

About feeling like if I took one break, I'd be back in the system by default.

Mark leaned forward. "Tristan, you still got prison time in your lungs. That kind of silence don't leave easy. But quiet don't mean you weak. It means you listening."

That hit. I realized I was so used to proving myself loud—I forgot to process myself soft. I'd made peace my enemy.

So I started doing something I never had time for:

Nothing.

Just... breathing.

Ten minutes a day. No clippers. No phone. No grind.

Just presence.

And from that silence came clarity:

I didn't need to do more.

I needed to do deeper.

Fewer gigs. More impact.

Fewer followers. More transformation.

Fewer fades. More foundation.

That night, I wrote Chapter 18 of the guide: "The quiet is not empty. It's full of truth. Listen harder."

Chapter 19:
Cutting Through the Static

There's always noise.

Social media.

Street talk.

City council.

Family expectations.

Your own doubts echoing like static in a busted speaker.

But when you're building something real, you gotta learn to cut through it.

I was cutting a client one day—young dude, fresh out.

He kept checking his phone like the world owed him an answer.

"You good?" I asked.

He shook his head. "Too much noise, man. Everybody saying what I should be doing. Nobody showing me how."

I stopped the clippers.

"You want the truth?"

He nodded.

"Block all that. Focus on *one* thing you can finish. Then finish it."

It sounded simple. But I knew it wasn't. Because I'd lived it.

The day my story hit a local TV station, my phone exploded.

Some loved it.

Some questioned it.

Some offered "opportunities" that smelled like exploitation.

And the haters?

They got louder too.

"This dude just tryna get rich off his record."

"He probably still dirty."

"Ain't nobody believe all that redemption talk."

At first, I wanted to clap back. Then I remembered what Tank told me back in Riverbend: "The loudest fools die first. Stay focused. Stay dangerous."

So I made a rule: If it didn't build me, my people, or my peace,

I tuned it out.

I doubled down on my classes.

Streamlined the guide.

Got with Isaac and Tasha and put together a toolkit—*The Cut Code*—for other barbers to use in reentry spaces.

I stopped doing ten things halfway and started doing three things excellently.

And the impact? It got louder than the hate ever could.

One day, Devon pulled me aside. "You ever think about how much noise you used to make?"

I laughed. "Yeah. Now I just sharpen blades."

He grinned. "You still loud, OG. Just... with purpose.

Chapter 20:
The Room They Said You'd Never Enter

The room smelled like old wood, policy, and pressure.

Downtown Nashville. Government plaza.

Not the kind of place they build for people like me.

But that day? I had a name tag. A suit. And a seat at the table.

Isaac invited me to speak on a panel about reentry entrepreneurship.

Lawmakers, nonprofit leaders, city council, and a few CEOs.

I looked around and realized—

Nobody in this room had ever done time.

But all of them had a hand in shaping what came after it.

I wasn't here to impress.

I was here to disrupt.

They gave me ten minutes.

I took fifteen.

I told them about porch cuts.

Zoning violations.

Clippers as curriculum.

Barbershop therapy.

My daughter's first words to me after thirteen years: "Hi."

I didn't sugarcoat. I said: "If you only give second chances to people with clean shoes and soft stories, you ain't building equity. You building a fantasy."

Silence. Then a councilwoman clapped. Then the room followed.

After the panel, a man in a thousand-dollar suit approached me. "We've got a funding program," he said. "We'd like to include your voice on the advisory board."

I looked him dead in the eye. "You want my story, or my strategy?"

He blinked. "Both, if you're willing."

That night, I stood in the shop and looked around.

Same chair.

Same cape.

Same mirror.

But everything was different.

I wasn't just in the room.

I belonged in it.

I wrote Chapter 20 of the guide: "They told you to stay in your lane. You built a highway."

Because they said I'd never be more than a felon.

But there I was—

A voice that couldn't be ignored.

A presence that couldn't be erased.

Chapter 21:
Borrowed Time, Full Price

I live on borrowed time.

Not borrowed like a favor.

Borrowed like debt.

Like every breath is a loan I'm still paying back to every day I wasted behind a number instead of a name.

One morning, I looked in the mirror and didn't recognize the man I was anymore.

Not because I'd changed.

Because I'd *evolved*.

The guilt was still there.

But now it stood next to growth, not in place of it.

I was 43.

Most men I did time with didn't see 30 free.

And if they did, they weren't living.

They were floating — ghosts with court papers and parole dates.

But me?

I was *living*.

Bleeding purpose.

Breathing proof.

Mama called that morning.

"You movin' too fast," she said. "You always been on fire, but baby... even fire needs rest."

She wasn't wrong.

I was tired again.

But not from the grind.

From the grief that never fully left.

I visited Tank's grave that weekend.

First time.

Didn't bring flowers. Just silence.

"Still here, big man," I said. "Still swingin'. Still building what they tried to keep buried."

I sat there for a full hour.

Didn't cry.

Didn't talk.

Just let myself feel *all* of it.

On the drive back, I pulled over and opened my notebook. I wrote: "Borrowed time don't mean borrowed dreams. If they gave you a second chance, make sure you live it loud enough to shake the people who bet against you."

Back at the shop, I told Devon and Jalen, "Take the clippers today. I'm just watching."

They looked nervous.

But they cut.

And I saw it then—

Legacy don't need your hands. It just needs your honesty.

Chapter 22:
No Apologies in the Mirror

There was a time I apologized for breathing loud.

For taking up space.

For daring to be seen.

For walking into a room with a record and a presence.

That time is over.

I used to flinch when people asked,

"So what do you do?"

I'd soften my answers.

"I cut hair."

"I write a little."

"I speak sometimes."

Now? I look them in the eye and say: "I change lives with clippers and conversation."

It took time to unlearn shame. Because this world will make you feel like survival requires silence.

But it doesn't.

It requires *truth*.

And truth don't whisper.

One day, a city official came to the shop. Said he'd seen my feature on the local news. Wanted to "understand the reentry perspective."

I offered him the chair.

He hesitated. Then sat.

I clipped his hair while he talked numbers. Budgets. Legislation. "At-risk youth."

I let him finish. Then I said: "You ever been afraid to check your mail because it might contain your own erasure?"

He blinked.

I kept going. "You ever walk into a room and know you're already guilty in their eyes—before you even say your name?"

He didn't answer.

I lined him up anyway.

Clean. Sharp.

No judgment.

At the end, he stood. Looked in the mirror. Said, "You have a gift."

I nodded. "Took me years to call it that."

That night, I stood in the same mirror after locking up. Looked myself dead in the eyes.

"I forgive you," I said to my reflection. "But I don't owe this world an apology for being built from broken."

Chapter 23:

Blueprints and Battle Scars

You don't build something real without bleeding for it.

Every blueprint I drafted came with a scar.

A lesson.

A moment I almost quit.

The second location almost folded in month three.

Plumbing issues.

Break-in.

Client no-show streak that hit like abandonment.

Loren looked at the books and said, "You sure we ain't doing too much?"

I didn't answer right away.

Because I wasn't sure.

I just knew I wasn't going backward.

So I did what I always did—tightened the plan.

Cut expenses.

Did late-night cuts for free just to rebuild traffic.

Partnered with a nearby gym—free cuts for new members.

It worked.

Barely. But it worked.

I used to think success was smooth.

Now I know—

It's jagged.

It's patched.

It's held together by grit and prayer.

And you feel every inch of it.

A former mentee came back to the shop.

Devon. Clean now. Barbering full-time.

He asked, "You still writing that guide?"

"Always," I answered.

He held up his forearm. Tattooed on it was one of my quotes: "Don't shrink. Shape.

I almost lost it right there.

Later that night, I looked at my own hands.

Calloused.

Strong.

Steady.

I traced the outline of a scar from prison—left thumb, old fight, years healed.

Then I looked around the shop. My blueprint. And realized—

Every scar I carried was part of the design.

Every setback had been structural.

And nothing I'd lost could outweigh what I was building.

Chapter 24:
Built From the South

Nashville raised me.

Not gently.

Not with soft hands.

But with callouses and codes, music and mess, red dirt and resistance.

The South don't ask who you are.

It tells you.

Tells you you're Black before you're human.

Tells you redemption is a myth.

Tells you to be quiet, be humble, be grateful you ain't in chains.

But I came to rewrite that script.

I wasn't running from Tennessee.

I was rising in it.

Making something from the soil they said wasn't ours.

Building chairs on porches and platforms in barbershops.

Speaking truth in rooms designed to ignore me.

And doing it all with Southern soul and Northern hustle.

Mama used to say, "A Southern man always got two jobs: survive the day and protect his dignity."

I used to think that meant staying out of sight. Now I know it means owning your light.

I was invited to speak at an education panel hosted by Fisk.

Professors. Lawmakers. Youth leaders.

They called it:

"Southern Roots: Modern Resistance."

I smiled when I read the flyer.

Because I knew I wasn't the face they expected.

But I *was* the voice they needed.

I opened my speech with this:

"I didn't rise despite Tennessee.

I rose through it.

The heat. The laws. The whispers.

I'm not just built from the South.

I'm built for it."

Silence.

Then an ovation.

One student asked me, "How do we change a place that don't want to change?"

My answer: "You build something so undeniable they either join you or get out the way."

That night, I looked out at Jefferson Street.

The old soul food spot.

The church.

The shop lights glowing against dusk.

And I felt peace.

Not because it was easy.

But because I knew—

Every brick I laid was rooted in home.

Not escape.

But elevation.

Chapter 25:
The Dream, Reconstructed

They told us the dream was dead.

Or delayed.

Or denied.

Or just not meant for people like us.

But I'm still dreaming.

Not because I'm naive—

Because I'm necessary.

The American Dream ain't a house on a hill or a white picket fence.

It's being able to walk into your own shop,

Look at the faces you've mentored,

And know you built a life no system could erase.

I sat in the chair one morning before opening.

Alana walked in with a coffee.

Devon followed behind her.

Jalen mopped the floor.

Mark called.

Isaac texted.

Tasha sent a flyer for our next panel.

The room was full of life I'd helped spark.

The man I was?

Gone.

The man I am?

Still writing. Still cutting. Still fighting.

I walked over to the mirror.

Same one I looked in when I first came home.

Back then, I saw shame.

Today?

I saw a man in motion.

I pulled the last printed copy of *The Free Man's Manual* off the shelf. Opened to the final page. Wrote this in pen: "The dream ain't dead. It just ain't theirs anymore. It's ours. And we rebuild it every time we love louder than fear."

That afternoon, I taught a class in the new Eastside space.

Ten students.

One projector.

And a message: "You don't have to be perfect to build.

You just have to begin."

They clapped.

But I wasn't looking for applause.

I was building architects.

The American Dream?

It's in every cut.

Every speech.

Every clapback.

Every time I get up and do it again.

It's not a fantasy.

It's real.

And it's under reconstruction—by people like me.

Final Reflection

Growth is not always visible in the moment, but the steps you've taken are real. Keep pushing, keep believing.

Quick Journal Prompt

What parts of your past do you now see as strength? How will you use them to help others?

Personal Challenge

Write down three habits you want to break and what you'll do daily to change them.

Quote

"The only thing standing between you and your goal is the story you keep telling yourself." — Jordan Belfort

From the Author

Thank you for taking this journey. Your story is still being written, and the best chapters are ahead.

www.ingramcontent.com/pod-product-compliance
Lightning Source LLC
Chambersburg PA
CBHW060406030726
47497CB00003B/868